The Tiara Club

at Ruby Mansions

For my very own Princess Jessica,
with MUCH love x x x
VF

www.tiaraclub.co.uk

ORCHARD BOOKS
338 Euston Road, London NW1 3BH
Orchard Books Australia
Level 17/207 Kent St, Sydney, NSW 2000

A Paperback Original
First published in Great Britain in 2007
Text © Vivian French 2007
Cover illustration © Sarah Gibb 2007
Illustrations © Orchard Books 2007

A CIP catalogue record for this book is available
from the British Library.

ISBN 978 1 84616 291 6

1 3 5 7 9 10 8 6 4 2

Printed in Great Britain

The paper and board used in this paperback are natural
recyclable products made from wood grown in sustainable
forests. The manufacturing processes conform to the
environmental regulations of the country of origin.

Orchard Books is a division of Hachette Children's Books

www.orchardbooks.co.uk

The Tiara Club
at Ruby Mansions

Princess Jessica

and the Best-Friend Bracelet

By Vivian French

ORCHARD BOOKS

The Royal Palace Academy
for the Preparation of Perfect Princesses

(Known to our students as "*The Princess Academy*")

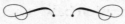

OUR SCHOOL MOTTO:
*A Perfect Princess always thinks of others
before herself, and is kind, caring and truthful.*

**Ruby Mansions offers a complete education for
Tiara Club princesses with emphasis on the
creative arts. The curriculum includes:**

*Innovative Ideas for our
Friendship Festival*

*Ballet for Grace
and Poise*

*Designing Floral
Bouquets
(all thorns will be
removed)*

*A visit to the Diamond
Exhibition
(on the joyous occasion of
Queen Fabiola's birthday)*

**Our headteacher, Queen Fabiola, is present at all times,
and students are well looked after by the head fairy
godmother, Fairy G, and her assistant, Fairy Angora.**

Our resident staff and visiting experts include:

*KING BERNARDO IV
(Ruby Mansions Governor)*

*LADY HARRIS
(Secretary to Queen Fabiola)*

*LADY ARAMINTA
(Princess Academy Matron)*

*QUEEN MOTHER MATILDA
(Etiquette, Posture and
Flower Arranging)*

We award tiara points to encourage our Tiara Club princesses towards the next level. All princesses who win enough points at Ruby Mansions will attend a celebration ball, where they will be presented with their Ruby Sashes.

Ruby Sash Tiara Club princesses are invited to go on to Pearl Palace, our very special residence for Perfect Princesses, where they may continue their education at a higher level.

PLEASE NOTE:
Princesses are expected to arrive at
the Academy with a *minimum* of:

*TWENTY BALLGOWNS
(with all necessary hoops,
petticoats, etc)*

TWELVE DAY DRESSES

*SEVEN GOWNS
suitable for garden parties,
and other special
day occasions*

TWELVE TIARAS

*DANCING SHOES
five pairs*

*VELVET SLIPPERS
three pairs*

*RIDING BOOTS
two pairs*

*Cloaks, muffs, stoles, gloves
and other essential
accessories as required*

Hi! It's me! Princess Jessica!
And it's lovely to meet you, and to
know you're here at Ruby Mansions with
me and my friends from Poppy Room.
Have you met us all? As well as me there's
Chloe, Olivia, Lauren, Georgia and Amy.
And Charlotte, Katie, Daisy, Alice, Sophia
and Emily are in Rose Room right next
door to us. Things would be just
about perfect if only those horrible
twins, Diamonde and Gruella weren't
here – they get worse and worse,
especially Diamonde!

Chapter One

"I just WISH I knew where it was," Amy said for about the twentieth time that morning, and Chloe, Olivia and I nodded sympathetically.

We were sitting in the homework room trying to finish our maths, but Amy had lost her watch and we weren't really concentrating.

"Could you have left it in the cloakroom?" Olivia asked.

Amy shook her head. "I've looked EVERYWHERE. It's completely disappeared."

I was about to suggest looking in her pockets when Lauren rushed in. "Have you heard?" she asked. "There's going to be a Festival of Friendship! Fairy G told me! And there's a competition before that too! We've got to think of something special to do for our friends, and the dormitory with the best idea gets to ride at the head of a Friendship Procession all the way round the town!"

"Ride?" Chloe sat up very straight. "You mean, actually riding on a pony?"

Lauren nodded, and her eyes were sparkling. "Isn't it just BRILLIANT? The stables are just FULL of the sweetest little dapple grey ponies – oops!" Lauren clapped her hand over her mouth. "Fairy G told me not to tell! It's meant to be a surprise!

Oh, we absolutely HAVE to win! Do hurry up, and then we can make our plans!"

And she dashed off again.

We looked at each other. "It does sound amazing," I said. "Dapple grey ponies! Won't they be gorgeous?"

"And we ought to win, because we Poppy Roomers are the best friends EVER," Olivia added.

Chloe sucked the end of her pencil. "I hope the ponies aren't too frisky. Just imagine falling off in front of a whole crowd of people! Wouldn't it be mortifying?"

"You'll be OK," I said. "Riding's easy!"

Amy looked at me. "Actually," she said, "it isn't easy if you're scared." She bit her lip. "Can I tell you a secret? I fell off a pony when I was little, and I've been terrified of riding ever since. I still have nightmares about it...it was HORRIBLE!"

"Didn't they make you get straight back on?" I asked. "They did me."

Amy turned very pink. "My mother wouldn't let me," she said. "And PLEASE don't tell anyone else! Please! If we win

I'm going to try REALLY hard to be brave..."

Of course we all promised. Perfect Princesses NEVER tell each other's secrets.

"Actually, Fairy G would never make you ride unless you wanted to," Chloe said. (Fairy G's our Fairy Godmother, and she looks after us.) "And we may not win anyway. Let's get this homework finished, and then we can meet up with Lauren and Georgia and think of some ideas."

"And ask them if they've found my watch," Amy said. "Although I don't think I'll ever see it again."

I looked at my maths book, and groaned. "How on EARTH are we supposed to know how much it costs to clean the palace windows?"

16

"What about putting, 'It depends how many windows there are?'" Olivia suggested.

"I think that's really clever," I said.

The others agreed, and we tidied
our notebooks into our lockers
and hurried off. I was last, and it
was only as I was about to go
through the door that I noticed
the twins. They were lurking in
the corner of the homework
room, almost hidden behind
a bookcase. They were whispering

together, and looking SO pleased
with themselves. I couldn't help
thinking they'd been spying on us,
but I told myself, "*A perfect
princess always thinks the best
of others.*" I ran after my
friends – and tripped over the rug
as I reached the corridor.

WHAM!

It took my breath away, and I felt SO silly. I picked myself up as quickly as I could, and that's when I saw Amy's watch lying in a corner. I let out a whoop of joy – Amy would be THRILLED to see it again! I put it in my pocket, dusted myself down and zoomed off.

Chapter Two

When I came hurrying into the recreation room Georgia was smoothing out a piece of paper. Chloe was clutching a pencil, and Lauren was leaning over her shoulder.

"Where's Amy?" I asked as I joined them.

"She's gone with Olivia to check

the noticeboard for the competition rules," Lauren explained.

"Here's Olivia now." Lauren waved as Olivia came puffing up and flung herself onto the sofa.

"We've got to think of 'Creative Ways to Make a Friend feel Special'," Olivia said. "And we don't just get to ride at the front of the procession if we win – we get ten tiara points each!"

I was beginning to wonder if Amy had gone to look for her watch upstairs. I was dying to see her face when I handed it over!

"Is Amy going to be long?" I asked.

Olivia shrugged. "I left her by the noticeboard," she said. "She was talking to Diamonde and Gruella—"

"I'll go and find her," I said,

"I've got SUCH a surprise
for her!" And I jumped up and
rushed off.

I absolutely flew down the
corridor, and I was lucky I didn't
meet any teachers – they'd have
given me a million minus tiara
points for running. I could see
Diamonde, Gruella and Amy by
the noticeboard, and I bounced up
to them.

"Guess what!" I said to Amy.
"Look what I found!" And I held
out her watch.

"THANK YOU!" Amy said,
and she took it, and waved it at
Diamonde. "Isn't it wonderful to

have friends who look after you?"
Diamonde turned towards me,
and I saw her wink at Gruella.

"Yes," she said, and she looked REALLY nasty. "It's wonderful to have friends – if they really ARE friends. But you see, Amy, we've got something we feel we ought to tell you about Jessica." And she shook her head as if she was very upset. "Isn't that right, Gruella?"

Gruella nodded. "That's right, Diamonde."

"Amy," Diamonde went on, "I'm afraid Jessica told us your secret. She told us you're a poor little scaredy cat, and you're EVER so scared of riding!"

I was so taken by surprise

I couldn't say a word. I just stared at Diamonde.

And then the most dreadful thing happened. Amy looked at me, and her eyes filled with tears.

"How COULD you?" she asked. "I didn't think you'd EVER do something like that. I really really didn't...!" She gave a little sob, and ran away down the corridor.

Diamonde smiled triumphantly.

"And we thought you were SUCH special friends," she said. "Oh dear!" And then she and Gruella marched off in the other direction, sniggering.

I was SO angry, and really upset as well. How could Amy think I'd do something so horrible? She was my friend. I'd NEVER tell any of her secrets. I took a deep breath, and walked slowly back to the recreation room.

As soon as I got through the door I knew they'd been talking about what had happened. Amy was sitting on a sofa, and Lauren and Georgia had their arms round

her. As I came towards them Amy
sniffed, and buried her nose in her
hankie. Chloe glared at me.

"Honestly, Jessica," she said.
"How COULD you be so mean?
Amy says you told the twins
about how she's scared of
riding – and you PROMISED you
wouldn't tell!"

"But I didn't!" I protested. "REALLY I didn't!"

Olivia shook her head. "I'm sorry, Jess," she said. "It must have been you. How else could they have known? Amy only told us ten minutes ago in the homework room!"

I had a sudden flash of inspiration.

"But the twins were there too! I saw them as I was going out – they must have overheard us talking! They were behind the bookcase!" Even as I explained, my voice died away. I could see from my friends' faces they SO didn't believe me.

Chloe frowned. "*I* didn't see them there." She turned to Olivia. "Did you?"

Olivia shook her head again. "No," she said.

Amy gave me SUCH a sad look. "I'm sure you didn't mean to tell," she said. "I expect it just sort of slipped out...and then the twins made the most of it."

I began to feel sick. Ever since I'd been at the Princess Academy I'd been best friends with everyone in Poppy Room...and now Lauren was looking at me as if I was as nasty as Diamonde!

Amy blew her nose hard. "Let's try and forget about it," she said

bravely. "If I wasn't so stupid about riding it would never have happened. Let's think about what we're going to do for the competition."

"You're a Perfect Princess," Chloe said, and gave Amy a hug. "You really truly are!"

"That's right." Olivia gave me a frosty look. "And I think Jessica should say she's sorry."

"But I haven't DONE anything!" I said, and then I couldn't help it. I burst into tears, and ran out of the room. And no one ran after me, and I knew why. They thought I was crying because I was guilty – but I wasn't. I was crying because they didn't believe in me.

Chapter Three

I rushed to the cloakroom, so nobody would see me, but when I got there Emily was washing her hands.

"Are you OK?" she asked.

I swallowed, and nodded. "I'm fine," I said, and I blew my nose hard. Emily looked at me doubtfully.

"Are you sure?" she asked.

"Yes, thank you." And I almost was. When things go wrong I like to DO things, and I'd thought of something. I'd go to the library, and find the most brilliant idea for the Friendship Festival competition, and a bit of me was thinking, "That'll show them!"

I was about to march out of the cloakroom when Emily called me back. "I'm so sorry," she said, "but could you tie up my bracelet for me?"

"Of course," I said, and I took the bracelet from her. "Oh! Isn't it pretty?"

Emily smiled. "It's a friendship bracelet," she said. "Daisy made it for me in the holidays, and I always wear it."

I nearly hugged her. FRIENDSHIP BRACELETS!

Wouldn't that be the best idea ever? But then I wondered if Emily had thought of it for Rose Room.

"No," she said when I asked her. "We're going to suggest making feathery fans. Don't say I told you!"

"I won't," I promised, and as I hurried away I felt SO much better. I was about to head back to the recreation room, but then I had another idea – why didn't I see if I could make a bracelet all by myself? And then I could show the others!

I practically skipped up to the craft room, and I was in luck.

The door was open, and Fairy Angora (she's our deputy fairy godmother) was tidying up. She looked a bit surprised to see me, but all she said was, "Can I help, my darling?"

"Yes PLEASE!" I said. "I want to make a Friendship Bracelet!"

Fairy Angora smiled. "Now THAT'S a good idea!"

"I know," I said. "But I want to try one out first."

The next hour or so whizzed by. Fairy Angora showed me where things were, and I made the SWEETEST friendship bracelet! It had pink

twinkly beads, and tiny pink hearts, and a dear little silver clasp shaped like two hands holding each other.

"Thank you VERY much," I said when it was finished.

"Aren't you going to wear it?" Fairy Angora asked.

I hesitated. "I don't think so," I said. Somehow it felt as if it might be bad luck to wear the bracelet before I'd sorted things out with my friends.

Fairy Angora smiled at me. "I see. Good luck!"

For a moment I wondered if she knew what had happened

between Amy and me, but she couldn't have. All the same, it was strange.

The bedtime bell rang while I was walking back, so I made my way up to Poppy Room.

Do you know what it's like when you come into a room, and everybody suddenly stops talking, and you just KNOW they were talking about you? Well, that's what happened to me.

Then Chloe said, "We've been deciding what we're going to suggest for the competition. We thought our idea could be to make pretty little cushions, and they'll be EXACTLY the right size to put a tiara on! What do you think?"

"I was wondering about friendship bracelets," I said, and I held mine out.

"Oooh!" Georgia's eyes lit up, and I saw Olivia smile, but Chloe shifted from foot to foot as if she was embarassed.

"Erm...I think we'd sort of decided on the little cushions," she said.

"That's right." Lauren folded her arms. "It was Amy's idea, and we thought it might cheer her up if we chose it." She gave me a meaningful sort of look. "She's still really upset."

The sick feeling in my stomach suddenly got worse. "Oh," I said. And I put my bracelet quickly in my pocket.

*

I didn't sleep at all well that night.
It was SO strange. I absolutely
knew I hadn't told the twins
about Amy being scared of riding,
but I still felt as if I'd done
something terrible.

"But I HAVEN'T," I told myself
firmly. "I really really haven't..."

At last I drifted off to sleep,
and I had all kinds of weird
dreams...and then the alarm went
off, and it was time to get up...

Chapter Four

The day didn't start well. No one talked to me at breakfast. When I walked into the dining room, I found there wasn't a seat for me at our usual place. I had to go and sit by myself.

Diamonde and Gruella looked at me and immediately started

giggling. "Look!" Diamonde sneered. "What's happened to the Poppy Roomers?"

Gruella put her head on one side. "I wonder why nobody's talking to Jessica? Aren't Poppy Roomers supposed to be the Best Friends Ever?"

"That's right," Diamonde chortled. "So they're BOUND to get to ride at the head of the Friendship Procession..."

"And then poor Amy will fall off her dear little pony!" Gruella just about fell off her chair, she was laughing so much.

I didn't know WHAT to do.
I stared at the table in front of me,
and did my best to ignore them.
The very next moment the door
burst open, and Fairy G came
billowing into the room.

Now, my dears," she boomed, "Time for the competition to see which dormitory has the best idea for 'Creative Ways to Make a Friend Feel Special'! Lily Room, what have you thought of?"

Princess Hannah stood up. "We've thought of embroidering hankies," she said, "with little tiaras in each corner."

Fairy G said, "Fine! Fine! And what about Tulip Room?"

Tulip Room said their idea was to spend every Monday morning polishing their friends' tiaras, and Sunflower Room wanted to arrange a special Friendship Tea

Party. Then Gruella burst out, "You haven't asked US, Fairy G!"

"That's right." Diamonde tossed back her hair. "We've got the BEST idea ever. We're going to give every princess in the school our autograph!"

"So when we're famous they'll be able to frame it," Gruella added.

Fairy G didn't look very impressed. She said, "I see. Now, let's hear from Rose Room."

Emily told her about making fans. Fairy G nodded. "And what about Poppy Room? Have you got a sparkling idea to make your friends feel really special?"

"THEY don't deserve to win, Fairy G," Diamonde interrupted rudely. "They're not even speaking to Jessica!"

"That's right!" Gruella chipped in. "WE should be riding those dapple grey ponies, not THEM!"

Fairy G gave Gruella the oddest look. "Princess Gruella," she said, and something in her voice made us all sit up very straight and pay attention, "might I ask how you know what colour the ponies are?"

"Lauren said they were dapple grey!" Gruella smirked. "We both heard her, didn't we, Diamonde? When we were in the homework room – OW!"

She stopped with a squeal. Diamonde had pinched her.

All my friends from Poppy Room GASPED – and stared at me – and began to talk all at once.

Fairy G began to swell, which is what she always does when she's angry.

"JUST WHAT IS THE
MEANING OF THIS?" she
bellowed.

Amy stepped forward, and sank
into a deep curtsey. "Fairy G," she
said, and her voice was shaking.
"I don't think ANY of us from
Poppy Room deserve to ride in
the Friendship Procession...except
Jessica." She looked round at
Lauren and the others.
"We...we've just been the worst
friends EVER to poor Jess, and
I want to tell her how very VERY
sorry I am." She walked over to
me, and took my hand. "Will you
ever forgive me?"

I blushed BRIGHT red. "Of course," I mumbled.

"POPPY ROOM!" Fairy G's voice was so loud I jumped. "KINDLY explain!"

Chloe put her hand up. "Please, Fairy G," she said, "Amy told us a secret, and we didn't know the twins were hiding in the homework room, and overheard. And then they told Amy it was Jessica who had told them..."

Olivia nodded. "Jessica did say she'd seen them in the homework room, but we didn't believe her—"

"But Jessica couldn't have seen us!" Gruella squealed. "We were hiding behind the bookcase!"

Fairy G gave Gruella a piercing look. "And WHY was that, Gruella?" she asked.

Gruella hung her head, and didn't answer.

"Diamonde? Can you tell me?" Fairy G asked, but Diamonde wouldn't say anything either. She stared hard at the table in front of her, and picked at her fingernail.

Fairy G folded her arms. "One of the most important things

about being friends," she said, "is to be able to sort out misunderstandings, and say sorry. Jessica, what do you have to say?"

"All I have to say," I said, "is that I've got the best friends in all the world!"

"Excellent," Fairy G said. "Now, what have YOU to say, Diamonde and Gruella?"

There was a long silence, and then the twins muttered, "Sorry."

"That's THAT dealt with," Fairy G said. She looked at Amy. "Now, I never did get to hear what Poppy Room's idea to make their friends feel special was?"

Amy, Chloe, Lauren, Olivia and Georgia looked at each other, and then at me. "Friendship bracelets!" they said, all together.

"Very good," Fairy G said. "A splendid idea."

An idea popped into my head.

"Excuse me," I said, "but could we make bracelets for Diamonde and Gruella too?"

Fairy G raised her eyebrows. "May I ask why?"

"Because they need to know

how to be friends more than any of us," I said, and I could feel myself blushing all over again.

"Well said." Fairy G smiled her huge beaming smile. "And for that answer, I declare Poppy Room the winners! Poppy Room will ride at the head of the Friendship Procession on dapple grey ponies!"

Chapter Five

The Festival of Friendship was WONDERFUL. By the time it arrived I was so tired of my friends telling me how sorry they were I had to tell them we WOULDN'T be friends if they ever mentioned it again!

And guess what? Fairy G tapped my bracelet with her wand – and suddenly there were EIGHT of them. One for each of us, and two for Diamonde and Gruella – who did NOT say thank you.

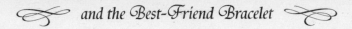

Amy was fine – it turned out
that Fairy G was going to ride
in the sweetest silver carriage,
together with Fairy Angora, and
they asked if Amy would be kind

enough to keep them company.
We went round and round the
town, bowing and smiling and
waving until I thought my arm
would drop off!

And then at the very end of the day there was a HUGE picnic beside the Princess Academy lake, with music and dancing. The trees were hung with sparkly fairy lights, and Chinese lanterns shone over the tables piled high with the most delicious things to eat – and there were heaps and heaps of sweet little pink satin cushions to sit on. We wore our most summery ball gowns, and we danced and danced until the sky was deep velvety blue, and sprinkled with thousands of tiny silver stars.

But the best moment came as I was going up to Poppy Room at the end of the day. Gruella was leaning against the wall outside the door, and as I walked past she pushed something into my hand.

"Sorry," she grunted, and then she was gone.

When I looked down, I found I was holding a little note. It said,

> Thanks for the bracelet, Jessica. Wish you were my best friend. It would be easier to be nice if you were.
>
> G.

And when I was lying in bed that night, I was SO happy, because I had so many wonderful friends…and I'm SO glad you're my friend too!

What happens next?
Find out in

Princess Georgia

and the Shimmering Pearl

Hello – and I'm very pleased to meet you!
I'm Princess Georgia, and Chloe, Jessica,
Olivia, Lauren and Amy share Poppy Room
with me – and we're very best friends.
We're trying to be REAL Perfect
Princesses, but – guess what!
It isn't always easy!
I'm so glad you're here at Ruby Mansions
with us – but do watch out for the
horrible twins, Diamonde and Gruella.
They're SO mean.
But we'll look after you.
You're our friend!

Win a Tiara Club
Perfect Princess Prize!

Look for the secret word in mirror writing that is
hidden in a tiara in each of the Tiara Club books.
Each book has one word. Put together the six words
from books **13** to **18** to make a special Perfect
Princess sentence, then send it to us together with
20 words or more on why you like the Tiara Club
books. Each month, we will put the correct entries
in a draw and one lucky reader will receive a magical
Perfect Princess prize!

Send your Perfect Princess sentence,
at least 20 words on why you like the Tiara Club,
your name and your address on a postcard to:
THE TIARA CLUB COMPETITION,
Orchard Books, 338 Euston Road,
London, NW1 3BH

Australian readers should write to:
Hachette Children's Books,
Level 17/207 Kent Street, Sydney, NSW 2000.

Only one entry per child.
Final draw: 31 May 2008

By Vivian French
Illustrated by Sarah Gibb
The Tiara Club

PRINCESS CHARLOTTE
AND THE BIRTHDAY BALL   ISBN   978 1 84362 863 7
PRINCESS KATIE
AND THE SILVER PONY   ISBN   978 1 84362 860 6
PRINCESS DAISY
AND THE DAZZLING DRAGON   ISBN   978 1 84362 864 4
PRINCESS ALICE
AND THE MAGICAL MIRROR   ISBN   978 1 84362 861 3
PRINCESS SOPHIA
AND THE SPARKLING SURPRISE   ISBN   978 1 84362 862 0
PRINCESS EMILY
AND THE BEAUTIFUL FAIRY   ISBN   978 1 84362 859 0

The Tiara Club at Silver Towers

PRINCESS CHARLOTTE
AND THE ENCHANTED ROSE   ISBN   978 1 84616 195 7
PRINCESS KATIE
AND THE DANCING BROOM   ISBN   978 1 84616 196 4
PRINCESS DAISY
AND THE MAGICAL MERRY-GO-ROUND   ISBN   978 1 84616 197 1
PRINCESS ALICE
AND THE CRYSTAL SLIPPER   ISBN   978 1 84616 198 8
PRINCESS SOPHIA
AND THE PRINCE'S PARTY   ISBN   978 1 84616 199 5
PRINCESS EMILY
AND THE WISHING STAR   ISBN   978 1 84616 200 8

The Tiara Club at Ruby Mansions

PRINCESS CHLOE AND THE PRIMROSE PETTICOATS	ISBN	978 1 84616 290 9
PRINCESS JESSICA AND THE BEST-FRIEND BRACELET	ISBN	978 1 84616 291 6
PRINCESS GEORGIA AND THE SHIMMERING PEARL	ISBN	978 1 84616 292 3
PRINCESS OLIVIA AND THE VELVET CLOAK	ISBN	978 1 84616 293 0
PRINCESS LAUREN AND THE DIAMOND NECKLACE	ISBN	978 1 84616 294 7
PRINCESS AMY AND THE GOLDEN COACH	ISBN	978 1 84616 295 4
CHRISTMAS WONDERLAND	ISBN	978 1 84616 296 1
BUTTERFLY BALL	ISBN	978 1 84616 470 5

All priced at £3.99.
Christmas Wonderland and *Butterfly Ball* are priced at £5.99.
The Tiara Club books are available from all good bookshops, or can be ordered direct
from the publisher: Orchard Books, PO BOX 29, Douglas IM99 1BQ.
Credit card orders please telephone 01624 836000 or fax 01624 837033 or visit our
website: www.wattspub.co.uk or e-mail: bookshop@enterprise.net for details.

To order please quote title, author, ISBN and your full name and address.
Cheques and postal orders should be made payable to 'Bookpost plc.'
Postage and packing is FREE within the UK
(overseas customers should add £2.00 per book).

Prices and availability are subject to change.

Look out for

Butterfly Ball

with Princess Amy and Princess Olivia!
ISBN 978 1 84616 470 5

Check out

website at:

www.tiaraclub.co.uk

You'll find Perfect Princess games and fun
things to do, as well as news on the Tiara
Club and all your favourite princesses!